White Wolves Series Consultant: Sue Ellis,
Centre for Literacy in Primary Education

This book can be used in the White Wolves Guided Reading programme
to help less confident readers in Year 5 gain more independence

First published 2007 by
A & C Black Publishers Ltd
38 Soho Square, London, W1D 3HB

www.acblack.com

Text copyright © 2007 David Calcutt
Illustrations copyright © 2007 Colin Paine

The rights of David Calcutt and Colin Paine to
be identified as the author and illustrator of this work
respectively have been asserted by them in accordance
with the Copyrights, Designs and Patents Act 1988.

ISBN 0-7136-8138-1
ISBN 978-0-7136-8138-3

A CIP catalogue for this book is available from the British Library.

This book is produced using paper that is made from wood grown
in managed, sustainable forests. It is natural, renewable and
recyclable. The logging and manufacturing processes conform
to the environmental regulations of the country of origin.

Printed and bound in Great Britain by MPG Books Limited

FOOL'S GOLD

David Calcutt
Illustrated by Colin Paine

A & C Black • London

Contents

Characters

Prospero   a doctor

Miranda   his daughter

Will   Prospero's servant

Mistress Snagge   a trickster

Captain Bombast   a trickster

Act One

Scene One

A room in **Prospero***'s house.*
Prospero *enters.* **Will** *follows, carrying
a large book.* **Prospero** *calls out. He
has a piece of cloth stuffed in each ear.*

Prospero Will! Will! Come here!

Will Here I am, master.

Will tries to walk in front of **Prospero***,
but* **Prospero** *turns away.*

Prospero Will! Where are you?

Will Right here, master!

Once again, **Prospero** *turns away.*

Prospero Will! Come here, I say!

Will I *am* here!

Miranda *enters.*

Miranda Father! What's the matter?
You're making a lot of noise.

Prospero Miranda! Have you seen
Will?

Miranda Will? He's just there –

Prospero Perhaps he's run away –
and taken my book! We must go
after him!

Miranda (*taking hold of* **Prospero**) Father! Listen to me! Will hasn't run off! And he hasn't taken your book!

Prospero Miranda! Something's happened to your voice! I can't hear it! A wicked spirit must have stolen it!

Will Master!

Will *tuggs at the back of* **Prospero***'s clothes.* **Prospero** *jumps in fright.*

Prospero Ah! Help! And now it's trying to drag me away!

Miranda There's no wicked spirit! You still have your earplugs in!

Prospero I can't hear you.

Miranda Look! (*She pulls the cloth from his ears.*) Can you hear me now?

Prospero Yes. How did they get there?

Miranda You put them in your ears every night when you go to sleep.

Will And you must have forgotten to take them out.

Prospero *sees* **Will** *for the first time.*

Prospero Will! There you are. I've been calling. Didn't you hear me?

Will I heard *you* all right.

Prospero Then why didn't you come? In bed, I suppose. Well, never mind about that now. We have work to do. Go and fetch my book.

Will It's here.

Prospero So it is. Come, then. There's no time to lose. Last night I dreamed I cracked an egg, and a bird flew out. And the bird's feathers were golden. You know what that means?

Will You have very strange dreams?

Prospero Fool! No, the dream was telling me that today is the day I shall find the secret of turning ordinary metal into gold! At last, after all this time, I shall do what no man has done! And we shall be rich! The richest people in the town! Come! We must set to work!

Prospero *goes.*

Miranda Will, before you leave. (*She holds out a small bag.*) Can you take this?

Will What's in it?

Miranda Money. I picked some herbs from our garden this morning and sold them in the market. Will

you put it with the rest of the money
I've been saving?

Will (*taking the bag from* **Miranda**)
Of course.

Miranda And remember to make
sure Father doesn't find it. If he does,
he'll spend it on his experiments.

Will You can trust me, Miranda.
He'll never find out where it's hidden.

Offstage, **Prospero** *calls.*

Prospero Will! Where are you?
I need my book!

Will I'd better go. But don't worry.
Your money's safe with me.

Will *goes.* **Miranda** *speaks to the audience.*

Miranda Poor Father. I wish he'd get this wild idea out of his head. He used to be a doctor, but ever since he read that book on alchemy he's given it all up. Now he spends his time doing experiments, and we just grow poorer and poorer. I hope he soon sees sense. If not, I don't know what will happen to us. Oh, it's a fool's dream to go searching for fool's gold!

Miranda *goes.*

Scene Two

*A quiet street near **Prospero**'s house.*

Snagge *and* **Bombast** *enter.*

Snagge It must be here.

Bombast It must. But where?

Snagge It must be near.

Bombast Perhaps down there.

Snagge We have to find it.

Bombast True, we must.

Snagge And find it soon.

Bombast If not, we're bust!

Snagge Then go and look!
Without delay!

Bombast All right, I'm going!
Straightaway!

Bombast *goes.* **Snagge** *speaks to the audience.*

Snagge These are hard times for people like us. There are so many laws! Sometimes we're locked in gaol. Sometimes we're chased out of town. Sometimes we're put in the stocks and people throw things at us! It's no wonder we turn to trickery to earn our daily bread. And what's the best sort of person to trick? A fool! And where can we find a fool? Right here in this town! We arrived this morning, and went to one of the taverns for a bite to eat. There, we overheard some of the locals talking about a man who's searching for the secret of making gold. So we asked a few questions, and found out where he lives –

Bombast *runs on.*

Bombast I've found it!

Snagge (*ignoring* **Bombast**) And as soon as my partner finds out where this house is –

Bombast I just told you, I have!

Snagge I'll be making gold out of him! Or my name isn't Mistress Snagge.

Bombast Mistress Snagge! Listen to me! I tell you, I've found it!

Snagge The house?

Bombast Yes. The one where that what's-his-name lives. The thingy man. That word I can't say.

Snagge Alchemist.

Bombast That's the one.

Snagge It's very easy. Try it.
Al – kem – ist.

Bombast It's no good. I have tried. I don't even know what it means.

Snagge It means fool. He thinks there's a way of turning ordinary metal into gold. And I'm going to show him how.

Bombast With our plan?

Snagge With *my* plan. And this stone. (*She takes a stone out of her pocket.*)

Bombast That's the stone somebody threw at me yesterday. It hit me on the head. It really hurt.

Snagge But today it will make us rich. Now, where *exactly* is this alchemist's house?

Bombast Just round the corner.

Snagge Have you found a way to get in?

Bombast The back door's unlocked.

Snagge Good. Do you have your costume?

Bombast Here, in my bag.

Snagge Then all is ready. You shall play your part, and I shall play mine. And if the fool plays his part, tonight you and I shall feast like kings!

They go.

Act Two

A room in **Prospero***'s house.* **Will** *runs on, carrying a small money box.*

Will Oh, dear! What am I going to do? Miranda keeps her money in this box. It's hidden in a hole in the wall behind a cupboard. I was putting the money into it when Prospero saw me!

Offstage, **Prospero** *calls.*

Prospero Will!

Will And now he's after me.

Prospero Will! Where are you?

Will He wants to know where the money's come from.

Prospero You can't hide from me!

Will And I don't know what to tell him!

Prospero *enters.*

Prospero There you are!

Quickly, **Will** *hides the box behind his back.*

Will Yes, master, here I am.

Prospero But where is *it*?

Will Where is what, master?

Prospero The box.

Will A box, master? What box?

Prospero The box you took from that hole. The box with money in it. I want to know where it came from!

Will I can't see a box with money in it, master.

Prospero You had it in your hand.

Will *brings one hand out from behind his back. He keeps the other hand, which holds the box, hidden.*

Will This hand, master?

Prospero Yes – that's the one!

Will There's no box in it now.

Prospero I'm sure there was.
Perhaps it was in your other hand!
Let me see!

Will *puts his hand behind his back,*
puts the box into it, then brings out
his other hand.

Will There. You see? Nothing.

Prospero *looks closely at* **Will**'s *hand.*
As he is doing this, **Snagge** *enters*
behind **Will**.

Prospero That's strange. I'm certain
I saw something.

Will Perhaps you were mistaken,
master.

Prospero Perhaps I was...

Snagge No, you weren't. The box is
behind his back.

Will *jumps round in surprise and*
Prospero *sees the box.*

Prospero (*to* **Snagge**) Thank you,
mistress.

Snagge It's my pleasure.

Prospero (*to* **Will**) Now, you had better tell me where this came from.

Will I... I can't...

Prospero Why not?

Will Because... I don't know...

Snagge He's lying. He must know.

Prospero That's right. You're lying. You must know.

Will I don't, master. It came to me in a dream. Like the one you had.

Prospero Did I have a dream?

Will Yes, master. You dreamed about

a golden bird coming out of an egg.

Prospero Ah, yes! My dream!

Will And *I* dreamed that there was a box hidden in a hole behind the cupboard. So I went and looked – and there it was.

Prospero Then this is wonderful! Marvellous! First there's my dream, and now there's yours! Now I feel sure that today I shall find the secret! At last, after all this time, I shall do what no man has done –

Snagge And so you shall.

Prospero (*to* **Snagge**) *I* know! But how do you? Who are you?

And what are you doing here?

Snagge My name is Mistress
Snagge. I know you will find the
secret, because I have it with me.
That's what I'm doing here.

Prospero But how do you know
what that secret is?

Snagge You are Master Prospero,
aren't you? The famous alchemist?
And you are searching for the secret
of turning ordinary metal into gold?

Prospero All that is true –

Snagge Then you're the man
I've been looking for. And here's
the secret *you've* been looking for.

(*She brings out the stone. It is wrapped in a special cloth.*) There!

Will What is it?

Snagge (*starting to unwrap the stone*) Something rare! (*She unwraps a little more.*) Something precious! (*She takes the cloth away.*) Something incredible! (*She holds up the stone.*)

Will It's a stone.

Prospero A stone?

Snagge A stone. But not just *any* stone. This is a *Dragon* Stone!

Prospero A Dragon Stone!

Snagge Yes! A Dragon Stone!

Will What's a Dragon Stone?

Snagge It's very rare. And it has special powers. First, you must crush it to powder. Then you mix that powder with other powders. Then you add water and heat the mixture. Then, when it's boiling, you put a piece of metal in. And –

Prospero The metal turns to gold!

Snagge That's right.

Prospero I must have that stone!

Snagge That's why I've brought it.

Prospero As a gift for me?

Snagge Not quite a gift.

Will (*to* **Snagge**) How do you come to have this Dragon Stone?

Snagge My husband is a sea captain. He brought it back from one of his voyages.

Prospero Do you want money for it?

Snagge Only a little –

Will (*to* **Snagge**) Why don't you use the Dragon Stone yourself?

Snagge Because only a true alchemist has the power to make it work.

Prospero And I am a true alchemist.

Snagge Indeed you are, sir. And if you can see your way to parting with a few pennies –

Will (*to* **Snagge**) How do we know this is a Dragon Stone? It looks just like an ordinary stone to me.

Prospero Will! Do you dare say this good woman may be lying to us?

Will I'm only asking, master.

Snagge And so he should. This could be an ordinary stone. I may be lying to you. But I can prove that I'm not. You may not believe me, but you must believe the spirit.

Prospero The spirit?

Snagge The spirit that guards the stone. The spirit that led me here to you. I shall summon it now...

Prospero A spirit! I'm not sure about this...

Will Neither am I...

Snagge Trust me, it's quite harmless. Just stand back while I make ready.

Prospero *and* **Will** *step back.*

Snagge Now I will call upon the spirit to appear! (*She chants.*)

> Huggle muggle,
> Jump and juggle,
> Wig and waggle, too.
> O, Dragon Spirit, come to us,
> We want to speak to you!

Bombast *leaps onstage. He is dressed in a red-and-white costume, hung with ribbons and bells, and wears a mask. He is carrying two flat pieces of wood, which he slaps together to make a loud noise.*

Bombast Boo!

Prospero *and* **Will** *jump in surprise.*

Prospero/Will Ah!

Snagge (*to* **Bombast**) Are you the spirit that guards this stone?

Bombast I am.

Snagge And is this a true Dragon Stone?

Bombast It is.

Snagge (*to* **Prospero**) Ask a question.

Prospero Er... does this stone have the power to turn metal into gold?

Bombast It does. But only one man may have that power.

Prospero And who is that man?

Bombast Prospero, the famous Al – Kem – Ist.

Prospero That's me!

Snagge Just as I said.

Will (*to* **Bombast**) I want to ask a question. If you're a spirit, why is there mud on your boots?

Bombast What?

Will And I don't think it's just mud. Pooh! It smells!

Snagge No more questions! The spirit is tired! (*She chants.*)

> Red as flame,
> White as snow,
> It's time for you
> To leave –

Bombast I go!

He slaps the pieces of wood together.

Prospero *and* **Will** *jump.* **Bombast** *runs quickly offstage.*

Prospero That is a Dragon Stone. And it must be mine!

Snagge It is yours. But if you could spare just one or two pennies for a poor old woman –

Prospero Of course –

Will He can't! He doesn't have any money. (*To* **Prospero**.) Don't you remember how poor we are?

Prospero Oh yes. (*To* **Snagge**.) I'm sorry, mistress. I don't have any money –

Snagge What's in that box?

Prospero The box! Of course! The money you dreamed about, Will. And now I know why. It was so I could reward this good woman for bringing me the Dragon Stone. (*Gives the box to* **Snagge**.) Here you are, mistress.

Snagge Thank you, sir. (*Gives the stone to* **Prospero**.) And here *you* are. I'm sure it will bring great wealth. And fortune. And fame. And now I must go. Farewell. Long may you prosper, O Prospero.

Snagge *goes.*

Prospero Come, Will. There is much to be done. First, we have to prepare the chemicals, then crush the stone,

then we must prepare the chemicals –
oh, I've already said that – er – and
then we must – it doesn't matter.
There are many things to be done
and we must begin straightaway!

Prospero *and* **Will** *go.*

Act Three

Scene One

The street outside **Prospero***'s house.*
Snagge *enters, looking for* **Bombast**.

Snagge Bombast! Where are you?
Bombast!

Bombast *enters behind* **Snagge**. *He is
still wearing his spirit costume and mask.*

Bombast I'm here.

Snagge *turns, sees* **Bombast**, *and
gives a cry of fright.*

Bombast What's the matter?

Snagge It's you! You're still wearing your costume. Take it off.

Bombast Oh, yes. Sorry. (*Takes off his costume.*) Well? Did it work?

Snagge It worked all right. The fool bought the stone. Look!

Snagge *shows the box to* **Bombast**.

Bombast Is that all he gave you?

Snagge Look inside.

Snagge *opens the box.* **Bombast** *gives a cry of delight.*

Bombast Money!

Snagge Enough to buy us a feast!

Bombast Two feasts!

Snagge A week of feasts!

Bombast I can't wait!

Snagge Then we'll go the tavern straightaway.

Snagge *and* **Bombast** *go.*

Scene Two

A room in **Prospero***'s house, a little while later.* **Miranda** *enters, carrying the food she has bought.*

Miranda Father! Will! I have some food! We can eat now.

Prospero *enters.*

Prospero Miranda! Where have you been?

Miranda Out buying some –

Prospero Food! Ah! Excellent. I'm so hungry.

Miranda There isn't much, I'm afraid –

Prospero It doesn't matter! Soon we'll have as much food as we want! The house will be filled with food! Overflowing with food! We'll need a bigger house! We'll buy a bigger house! We'll live in one house and keep our food in the other!

Miranda Father, are you all right?

Prospero I've never been better! Today is the day, Miranda!

Miranda What day?

Prospero The day I've dreamed of! And it was a dream that brought it to me! Two dreams!

Miranda What are you talking about, Father?

Prospero Look! Here it is! (*Puts his hand in his pocket.*) Well, it *was* here. (*Feels in his other pocket.*) It's gone!

Miranda What's gone?

Prospero (*searching his clothing*) I had it – and now – I can't have lost it. (*Calls.*) Will! Come here, quickly!

Will *enters.*

Will Master?

Prospero I can't find it! What am I going to do? It's gone!

Will (*holding up the stone*) I suppose you mean this.

Miranda What's that?

Prospero What do you think it is?

Miranda It looks like a stone.

Prospero It is. But it's not just *any* stone. It's a Dragon Stone! And with it I shall be able to turn ordinary metal into gold.

Miranda Where did you get it?

Prospero I bought it.

Miranda What with? We don't have any money.

Prospero That's what's so amazing! We did have money! It was in a box –

Miranda (*growing suspicious*) In a box...

Prospero It was hidden – but Will dreamed where it was!

Miranda Did he?

Prospero Tell her, Will. Tell Miranda about your dream.

Miranda Yes, Will. Tell me about your dream.

Will Well, you see… I… had this dream…

Prospero He dreamed about a chicken, and the chicken laid an egg, and the box of money was inside the egg – no, that's not right. I dreamed about an egg, and he dreamed about a chicken – no, a box, and the box

was full eggs – no, not eggs – what
was in the box?

Miranda Money.

Prospero Money! That's right! How
did you know? Did you dream about
it as well? Eggs and chicken and
money! It all comes to the same
thing! I was able to buy the Dragon
Stone. And now all our dreams will
come true! Come, Will! To work!

Prospero *goes.*

Miranda So, Will. You dreamed
about a hidden box, did you?
A box that had money in it.

Will Well...

Miranda It wouldn't be *my* money by any chance? The money I asked you to look after and keep safe!

Will I can explain –

Miranda It had better be good.

Prospero (*offstage*) Will!

Will But not now! I have to go and help your father.

Will *runs offstage.*

Miranda Will! Come back here! Now! Where's my money? And what's a Dragon Stone? Will somebody tell me exactly what's been going on!

She goes.

Scene Three

A room in **Prospero***'s house, the next
day.* **Prospero** *enters. He speaks aloud
to himself.*

Prospero I don't understand it. I've
done everything right. I crushed the
stone. I mixed some of it with the
powders. I boiled them in water until
they were dissolved. I put a piece of
metal in the liquid. And – nothing! It
didn't change! No gold! I tried again.
Nothing. And again. Nothing. And
again. Still nothing. All day and all
night, and still it hasn't worked.
There can only be one reason why.
I must be doing something wrong.
And I think I know what it is!

Will *enters,*
rubbing his eyes.

Will! Where have
you been?

Will Nowhere,
master. I fell
asleep.

Prospero Are
you awake now?

Will I think so.

Prospero Good. Because, listen, I
know what I've been doing wrong.

Will So do I.

Prospero Do you?

Will I tried to tell you right from the start. It's the –

Prospero Powders!

Will Powders?

Prospero That's right. We didn't use the right powders! You must go and buy some different ones.

Will But –

Prospero Wait here. I'll go and write a list of what you need.

Will Master – !

Prospero *goes.*

Oh! It's no good trying to talk to him. He won't listen to reason or see

56

sense! He's a dope! He's a –

Miranda *has entered.* **Will** *sees her.*

– lovely, kind, gentle old man.

Miranda That's right, Will. He is.
But he's also a fool. And that stone
he bought isn't a Dragon Stone, it's
a *Fool's* Stone.

Will You're right. And I was a fool
for letting him catch me with the
money. And for making up that story
about the dream. And for –

Miranda That doesn't matter now.
What matters is we have no food in
the house, and no money to buy any.

Will Can't you sell more herbs?

Miranda I picked the last yesterday. I don't know what's going to happen to us.

Prospero *enters with a piece of paper. He hands it to* **Will**.

Prospero Here you are. That's a list of all the powders I need. (*He sees* **Miranda**.) Miranda, is breakfast ready? I'm very hungry. (*To* **Will**.) Are you still here? Off you go and buy those powders! (*To* **Miranda**.) And hurry up with breakfast. I'm starving!

Prospero *goes*.

Miranda He's not the only one. We'll all be starving soon.

Will No, we won't. I know the man who runs the tavern in the market place. I'll ask him to give me a job cleaning tables and sweeping the floors. It won't pay much, but it will be enough to buy a little food.

Miranda You don't have to do that.

Will Yes, I do. It was my fault he found your money, and I'm going to make up for it.

Offstage, **Prospero** *calls.*

Prospero Miranda! Where's my breakfast?

Miranda I'd better go. I'll tell him breakfast is on its way.

Will And if not breakfast, supper. Whatever happens, I promise we won't starve!

Miranda *and* **Will** *go, separately.*

Act Four

Scene One

A tavern in the centre of town. **Snagge** *and* **Bombast** *enter.* **Bombast** *is eating a pie.*

Snagge I'm full! I couldn't eat another thing.

Bombast Mrmmffmrmmff.

Snagge What did you say?

Bombast Mrmmffmrmmff.

Snagge Swallow that pie. I can't understand you.

Bombast I said, I could. I could eat another pie. And another, and another, and –

Snagge I'm sure you could.

Bombast Give me some more money, then.

Snagge No. We've spent almost half of it already. We'll want to eat again tomorrow.

Will *enters, sweeping the floor.* **Snagge** *and* **Bombast** *don't see him.*

Bombast But what will we do the day after tomorrow?

Snagge We'll get some more money. Play the same trick again.

Bombast On the same old man?

Snagge No. There are plenty like him in the land. Fools who think they can make gold. All we need is another Dragon Stone – and they're lying all over the ground.

Bombast I can be the spirit again!
(He speaks as the sprit.)

Red as flame,

White as snow.

Snagge Give us your money

And off we go!

They both laugh and go. **Will** *speaks to the audience.*

Will So it was a trick! I guessed as much, but now I know for sure. I'll go and tell my master and Miranda straightaway. And then see if we can think of a way of getting the money back.

Will *goes.*

Scene Two

A room in **Prospero**'s *house, a little later.* **Prospero**, **Miranda** *and* **Will** *enter.*

Prospero What a fool I have been! To be tricked like that! She seemed such an honest woman! Didn't you think she seemed honest, Will?

Will Actually, no, I didn't.

Prospero Then why didn't you say?

Will I tried to –

Prospero But I wouldn't listen. Because I'm a fool! Miranda! I gave them all your money! (*To* **Will**.) You lied to me about that!

Miranda It wasn't Will's fault, Father. It was mine. I made him promise not to tell you about it.

Prospero It wasn't your fault, either. I'm to blame for everything!

Will No, you're not, master. It's those two tricksters who are to blame.

Prospero Yes! The villains! The rascals! Something should be done about them! Something will be done. But what? What can we do? If I accuse them of trickery, everyone will know what a fool I've been! The whole town will laugh at me! There's nothing we can do.

Miranda There might be something.

Will What?

Miranda I've just had an idea.

Prospero What is it?

Miranda It could work...

Will Tell us!

Miranda Then again –

Prospero Miranda!

Miranda It's worth a try, anyway.

Will I'm sure it is. But what is it?

Miranda It's a plan.

Prospero A plan!

Miranda A scheme.

Will A scheme!

Miranda To trick the tricksters.

Prospero Trick the tricksters!
Wonderful! I like that. Yes! We'll trick
the tricksters! Excellent idea!

Marvellous plan! Come! Let's put it into operation straightaway!

Prospero *goes*.

Will He likes your plan.

Miranda Yes.

Will The only trouble is, he doesn't know what it is yet.

Miranda I know. I'd better go and tell him.

Miranda *goes off after* **Prospero**.
Will *calls out*.

Will And neither do I! So you'd better tell me as well!

Will *runs off after* **Miranda**.

Scene Three

The tavern in the centre of town, that evening. **Snagge** *and* **Bombast** *enter.* **Bombast** *is groaning and holding his stomach.*

Snagge It's your own fault.

Bombast I know.

Snagge I did warn you.

Bombast You did.

Snagge But did you listen?

Bombast I didn't.

Snagge And now your stomach hurts.

Bombast And now my stomach *really* hurts.

Snagge So perhaps in future you'll listen to me.

Bombast No, I won't.

Snagge Why not?

Bombast Because I like pies!

Bombast *goes off, groaning.*

Snagge Fool! Sometimes I think I'd be better off without him. He does have his uses, but he will keep eating pies!

Miranda *enters.*

Miranda Mistress Snagge?

Snagge *jumps.*

Snagge What?

Miranda You *are* Mistress Snagge?

Snagge That depends on who wants to know.

Miranda I'm Miranda. Prospero's daughter. The alchemist. You gave him a stone yesterday – a Dragon Stone –

Snagge Sorry – that wasn't me – it was somebody else – I've got to go – goodbye –

Snagge *starts to run off.*

Miranda – and he's very grateful.

Snagge *stops.*

Snagge Grateful?

Miranda Of course he's grateful. Without the Dragon Stone he wouldn't have been able to make gold.

Snagge He's made gold?

Miranda Yes. A lot of gold. And to show his gratitude, he's going to make some for you.

Snagge I don't know what to say...

Miranda He'd like you to come round to our house tonight. Then he'll demonstrate the power of the Dragon Stone, and make you a gift of gold. You will come, won't you?

Snagge Yes, of course.

Miranda Good. Be there at nine o'clock. And prepare to be amazed!

Snagge I will... thank you...

74

Miranda Oh, no. It's *I* who should thank *you*.

Miranda *goes.*

Snagge It worked! How did it work? It was just an ordinary stone. Unless, by pure chance, we really did find a Dragon Stone! That must be it. And I sold it! But it won't be hard to get back. We'll go to the house tonight and receive our gold. I'll find out where Prospero keeps the stone. Then, when they're all asleep, we'll go back to the house and steal it! And then we'll make our fortunes!

Bombast *enters.*

Bombast I feel a bit better now.

Snagge Bombast, soon you're going to feel a lot better.

Bombast Am I?

Snagge Oh, yes. We're both going to feel better than we've ever felt before!

Snagge *and* **Bombast** *go.*

Act Five

A room in **Prospero**'s *house, that night.* **Prospero** *and* **Miranda** *enter.*

Miranda Now, Father, you must remember everything you have to do.

Prospero Of course, Miranda.

Miranda Good. It's almost nine o'clock. They should be here soon.

Prospero Who should be here?

Miranda Those tricksters. The ones who fooled you into buying the stone.

Prospero They're coming here? What for?

Miranda Oh, Father! You've forgotten our plan! And if you forget –

Prospero I haven't forgotten, Miranda. I was just having a little joke. My memory isn't that bad.

There's a knock at the door.

Miranda That will be them. Good. I'd better go and get ready.

Prospero Go? Where? And get ready for what?

Miranda Father!

Prospero Joking again. Off you go. I'll deal with these two.

Miranda *goes. There's another knock at the door.*

Come in! The door's not locked!

Snagge *and* **Bombast** *enter.*

Snagge Master Prospero! Greetings!

Prospero Mistress Snagge! How lovely to see you again!

Snagge The pleasure is all mine. This is my husband, Captain Bombast.

Prospero Ah, the man who brought

back the Dragon Stone from overseas. Very pleased to meet you, captain.

Bombast And I am very pleased that the Dragon Stone has made you rich. It has made you rich, hasn't it?

Prospero Oh, yes. Very rich. Very rich indeed. From the crushed stone I have made a mixture that has the power of turning ordinary metal into gold.

Snagge Just as I said it would.

Prospero And I want to reward you for bringing it to me.

Snagge That is so kind of you,

Master Prospero. But, please, you must only give us a small bag of gold.

Bombast (*quickly*) Each.

Prospero I shall give you more than that –

Snagge All right – if you insist –

Prospero I shall show you wonders! I shall show you marvels! I shall call up spirits!

Bombast Spirits?

Prospero Yes! The stone has given me power to call up spirits. And I shall call up some to speak to you.

Bombast I think we'll just take the gold –

Prospero No! You cannot go until you have spoken with the spirits! Don't move! I shall call them!

Prospero *raises his arms in the air and closes his eyes.* **Will** *enters, behind*

Snagge *and* **Bombast**, *dressed as a spirit.*

Snagge If it's all the same to you, Master Prospero, I think we'll just go.

Bombast (*to* **Snagge**) Go? But what about the gold?

Snagge Forget the gold. He doesn't have any. Can't you see?
He's gone mad.

Bombast So there won't be any spirits, either?

Snagge Of course not. (*To* **Prospero**.) Thank you very much, Master Prospero. (*To* **Bombast**.) Quick! Before he opens his eyes!

They turn to leave and come face to face with **Will***, dressed as a spirit.*

Snagge/Bombast (*together*) AH!!!

Will (*in a scary voice*) I am the Spirit of Water and Air,

Liars and cheats should all beware!

I'll hunt and chase them round about,

And shiver and shake them inside out!

Snagge/Bombast (*together*) Run!

They turn to run in the opposite direction, but as they do, **Miranda** *enters, dressed as a spirit.*

Snagge/Bombast (*together*) AH!

Miranda (*in a scary voice*) I am the Spirit of Earth and Fire,

Take care, beware, all cheats and liars!

I'll make them cringe, I'll make them croak,

And singe and sizzle them up in smoke!

Snagge/Bombast (*together*) Run!

They turn to run, but **Will** *is in front of them.*

Will I am the Spirit of Water and Air!

Snagge/Bombast (*together*) AH!

They turn again, but **Miranda** *is in front of them.*

Miranda I am the Spirit of Earth and Fire!

Snagge/Bombast (*together*) AH!

Snagge Run!

Bombast Run!

Snagge This way!

Bombast This way!

Snagge *and* **Bombast** *run in different directions but are stopped by* **Will** *and* **Miranda**. *They run back, bump into each other, and fall over. The money box drops onto the floor.*

Snagge Fool!

Bombast Fool yourself!

Will/Miranda (*together*)
WOOOOOOOOOO!

Snagge/Bombast (*together*) AH!

Snagge *and* **Bombast** *jump to their feet and run offstage.*

Will They've gone! The plan worked!

Miranda I hoped it would.

Will I knew it would!

Miranda (*picking up the money box and looking inside.*) And at least half the money is still here.

Prospero My thanks to both of you. I never knew I had such an intelligent daughter. Or such a faithful servant. I have been a very foolish old man. But no more! I shall give up the pointless search for gold, and return to being a doctor.

Will A much more sensible profession.

Miranda And a much more rewarding one.

Prospero The only thing is, I'm afraid you can no longer be my servant, Will.

Will (*disappointed*) Oh.

Miranda Why not, Father?

Prospero Because – he's going to be my assistant.

Will Your assistant, master?

Prospero Yes.

Will I'm going to be a doctor's assistant!

Prospero And you too, Miranda. All three of us will practise the art of medicine together.

Miranda No more spirits and spells, Father?

Prospero I promise, Miranda. No more spirits, no more spells.

Will Then everything has turned out well!

All three turn to the audience.

Miranda Yes, All has turned out well, it seems,
      No more chasing idle dreams.

Will Easy wealth and magic charms,

Such dreams can only bring us harm.

Prospero I've learned my lesson, and learned it well.

I'll burn my magic book of spells
Find out my book of medicine,

Become a doctor once again.

Will What started bad has ended good
And happily, as all stories should.

Miranda And so it's done, the tale is told
Of foolish dreams, and Fool's Gold.

The End

About the Author

David Calcutt writes plays for the theatre and radio. Many of his plays for young people have been published and are used in schools. He also writes stories and poems, and has just finished his first novel.

David lives near Birmingham with his wife, a grown-up daughter, and a dog. When he's not writing, David likes walking with his dog, cycling, reading, going to concerts, the theatre and cinema, and eating out. He's interested in myths, legends and folk tales, and often adapts the plots of these in his writing.

Other White Wolves Playscripts...

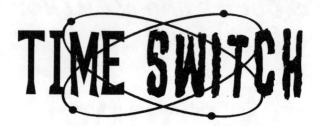

TIME SWITCH

Steve Barlow &
Steve Skidmore

When Bev and friends go to audition
at the Globe, they don't expect to be
spirited back to the year 1600. Plague
is sweeping London and Shakespeare's
company needs actors. But is Tim a
good choice to play Juliet? And can Bev
and Hayley prevent murder most foul
as a jealous rival plots his revenge?

Time Switch is a humorous play,
with parts for six people.

ISBN: 9 780 7136 8135 2 £4.99

Other White Wolves Playscripts...

Let's Go to London!

Kaye Umansky

A random group of travellers all
meet on the riverbank one morning,
all heading for London town. But when
the ferryman is too drunk to take them
across the river, there's only one thing
for it – they must walk! Little do
they know what an adventure
it will turn out to be!

Let's Go to London! is a humorous
play, with parts for six people.

ISBN: 9 780 7136 8151 2 £4.99

WHITE WOLVES

Year 5

The Path of Finn McCool • Sally Prue

The Barber's Clever Wife • Narinder Dhami

Taliesin • Maggie Pearson

Fool's Gold • David Calcutt

Time Switch • Steve Barlow and Steve Skidmore

Let's Go to London! • Kaye Umansky

Year 6

Shock Forest and Other Stories • Margaret Mahy

Sky Ship and Other Stories • Geraldine McCaughrean

Snow Horse and Other Stories • Joan Aiken

Macbeth • Tony Bradman

Romeo and Juliet • Michael Cox

The Tempest • Franzeska G. Ewart